I LOVE ME BECAUSE...

Printed in the United States of America
First Printing, 2021

Sean George Enterprises, LLC
3330 Cobb Parkway
Suite 324-251
Acworth, GA. 30101

To book Sean or purchase any of his products,
please visit our website at: Seangeorgeenterprises.com or
email us at: info@seangeorgeenterprises.com

I LOVE ME BECAUSE...

CREATED BY SEAN GEORGE, M.ED., MBA

ILLUSTRATED BY CAMERON WILSON

According to Ali McPherson in her article - A Black Woman's Guide to Self Love, "The first step to achieving self-love is to acknowledge and list all the things you love about yourself." "I Love Me Because…" is a book that was created to help young girls on their journey to reach self-love.

This book is dedicated to all the young girls, including the young girls inside older girls and women. Never forget that you are beautifully and wonderfully made. There are numerous reasons why you should love yourself and why you are worthy to be loved.

I love me because...

I love me because...

I love me because...

...I am Friendly...

I love me because...

I love me because...

I love me because...

...I am athletic...

I love me because...

...I am beautiful...

I love me because...

...I am unique...

CALL & RESPONSE AFFIRMATION

Parents, our daughters need support and affirmations in their journey to self love. As a result, I am asking you to, at least 2x's per week, participate in this Call & Response Affirmation with your daughter(s).

Parents: Who are You?

Daughter(s): I am an intelligent, talented, confident, caring, friendly, generous, helpful, athletic, beautiful, and a unique child who is blessed and highly favored.

ABOUT THE AUTHOR

SEAN GEORGE has been in education for 20 years; he holds teaching certificates in Mathematics, English/Language Arts, and Social Sciences, and he is the Founder/CEO of Sean George Enterprises, LLC. He is also the Founder/CEO of Ties That Make A Difference, Inc., a 501©3 nonprofit organization. Ties That Make A Difference, Inc. is a 501©3 nonprofit whose mission is: To tie together faith, family, and community in order to help all youth and young adults, especially those who are considered at-risk, to excel academically, make a difference in the world by blessing others, and discover and pursue their dreams and career goals using the Bible as the foundation. He also holds a Bachelor's of Arts (BA) degree in Mass Communications/ Public Relations from Morehouse College, a Master's of Education/ Mathematics (M.Ed.) degree from Cambridge College, and a Master's in Business Administration (MBA)/ Project Management degree from Walden University.

SEAN GEORGE lives with his wife Maritza and daughter Sanaa (A Sophomore at Spelman College) in Georgia. He also has three grown children: Shawn and Amanda, and a new daughter, Nicole, who is married to his son Shawn. Shawn and Nicole were blessed with a son, Trey; and Amanda and Ken were blessed with a daughter, Kyndal, making Sean an extremely proud grandfather.

OTHER BOOKS WRITTEN BY
SEAN GEORGE, M.ED., MBA

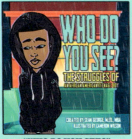

"WHO DO YOU SEE?"
SERIES BOOK 1

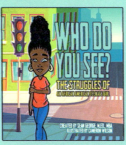

"WHO DO YOU SEE?"
SERIES BOOK 2

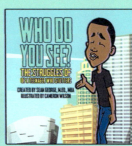

"WHO DO YOU SEE"
SERIES BOOK 3

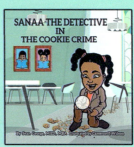

"SANAA THE DETECTIVE"
SERIES BOOK 1

"I NEED YOU"
SERIES BOOK 1

"I NEED YOU"
SERIES 2

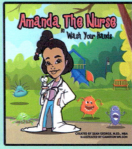

"AMANDA THE NURSE"
SERIES BOOK 1

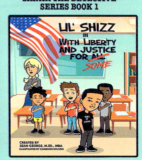

"LIL SHIZZ"
SERIES BOOK 1

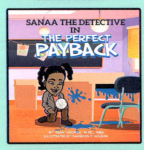

"SANAA DETECTIVE"
SERIES BOOK 2

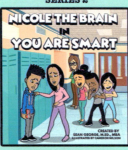

"NICOLE THE BRAIN"
SERIES BOOK 1

"I KNOW MY DAD"
SERIES BOOK 1

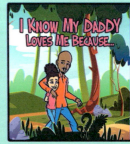

"I KNOW MY DAD"
SERIES BOOK 2

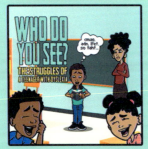

"WHO DO YOU SEE?"
SERIES BOOK 4

COMING SOON!

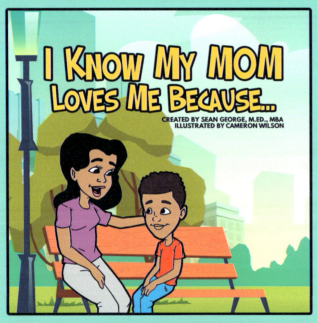

"I KNOW MY MOM..."
SERIES BOOK 1

"I LOVE ME BECAUSE..."
SERIES BOOK 2

Made in United States
Troutdale, OR
02/26/2025

29350702R00024